T0390209

PRAISE FOR
TIM LEBBON

"Just when you think Tim Lebbon is at the top of his game, he claws himself further up the tree." —DANIEL BARNETT, author of *Scuttler's Cove*

"Tim Lebbon is a master storyteller." —NUZOH NUZO ONOH, author of *Where the Dead Brides Gather*

"Lebbon is a master." —CHRISTOPHER GOLDEN, *New York Times* bestselling author of *Road of Bones* and *All Hallows*

"Bloody brilliant!" —JONATHAN MABERRY, *New York Times* bestselling author of *Cave 13* and *Empty Graves*

ALSO BY TIM LEBBON

Secret Lives of The Dead
Among the Living
The Last Storm
Eden
Coldbrook
The Silence

THE RELICS TRILOGY
Relics
The Folded Land
The Edge

DEAD RED AND RAZOR

TIM LEBBON

BAD HAND BOOKS

Dead Red & Razor
Copyright © 2025 by Tim Lebbon

Print ISBN: 979-8-9924837-2-7
eBook ISBN: 978-1-967846-14-6

Cover & Interior Illustrations by HagCult
Cover & Interior Design by Todd Keisling | Dullington Design Co.

No part of this work may be reproduced or transmitted in any form or by any means without permission, except for inclusion of brief quotations with attribution in a review or report. Requests for reproduction or related information should be addressed to the Contact page at www.badhandbooks.com.

Without in any way limiting the author's, artists', and publisher's exclusive rights under copyright, any use of this publication to "train" generative artificial intelligence (AI) technologies to generate text or imagery is expressly prohibited. The author and artists reserve all rights to license uses of their work for generative AI training and development of machine learning language models.

This is a work of fiction. All characters, products, corporations, institutions, and/or entities in this book are either products of the author's imagination or, if real, used fictitiously without intent to describe actual characteristics.

Bad Hand Books
www.badhandbooks.com

For KC

Dead Red Virgilio was tired, aching, and spattered with someone else's blood and brains, but with Flogging Molly blasting from the car speakers and the windows down, she found it easy to stay awake. The hot desert air helped, scoring sandpaper breaths across her exposed skin. It smelled of vast landscapes and wandering ghosts. She felt at home with both.

What also helped was where she was heading, and who she was going to kill when she reached her destination.

I had three kids, the voice said. *Two young twins, and a girl just finishing high school. Now they're without a daddy. Because of you. Three kids growing up without a father.*

"You were a bad man," Red said. "They're better off without you."

Bad? Who's bad? Get a load of you.

Red glanced in the rearview mirror. She hadn't slept in twenty hours, and tired eyes stared back. She pulled a tissue from her pocket and wiped at the gory remnants on her right cheek and jawline. They'd dried on, crisp and hard. She spat on the tissue and tried again, and some crumbled matter fell onto her shoulder.

"I'm not bad," Red said, and she heard a chuckle from the voice, and she remembered how that laughter had always made her happy and safe, and how Matty Van had held her in his arms so that his laugh passed through into her own chest.

Bad as they fucking come, his voice muttered. Keeping one eye on the road, she reached for the head on the passenger seat and rolled it into the footwell. It fell with a dull thud, face turned away from her and exposing the damage to its left side. That's where the brains had spilled from.

It hadn't surprised her when Nick Strand's decapitated head had started talking in her dead lover's voice. It happened every time, and she knew from experience the voice would grow quieter, quieter, until it faded once again into memory. Maybe this afternoon, but definitely by this evening. It was rare she went to bed with Matty's voice echoing in her head.

She mourned that. She missed him. But now, today, she might finally be able to lay his troubled soul to rest.

Maybe then he'd stop berating her from the corpses of the people she killed.

She glanced at the dashboard clock. It was midday; the sun blazed at its highest, and she wished she'd brought her sunglasses. She had planned on being back at her rented apartment by now, showering remnants of Nick Strand from her skin and the memory of his pleading, whiny voice from her mind. He'd killed thirteen people over the past seven years, most in cold blood, all of them because they'd challenged his position in the local crime hierarchy. Red didn't give a fuck about any of it. They were bad people, and she killed bad people for money. She looked at her profession as—

Doesn't that make you a bad person too?

"Shut up," she whispered. "Go to sleep." She once again considered throwing the head from the car. She'd leave it for the vultures and coyotes, the flies and ants, Strand finding his final resting place here in this arid place. That wouldn't stop her dear dead Matty whispering to her, but at least it'd mean the voice was only in her mind.

She glanced down at the head. It jittered as the car thunked over a dip in the hot road and rolled so that his pale left eye stared up at her. She expected him to say something else. He didn't. Maybe that look was enough, for now.

Red had to keep the head. Her employer for this hit had insisted on seeing Strand's chopped-off cabbage before he'd pay her the hundred grand bonus. Just this little detour and one of the most important loose ends of her life to sort out, and then she'd collect.

Her phone buzzed in the door pocket. She fished it out, glanced at the screen, and grimaced. River. For a second, she considered not answering, but River was the only one who really cared for her now that Matty was dead. She wouldn't dream of doing anything to make him worry more.

"Hey," she said, putting the phone on loudspeaker and resting it on one knee.

"It's gone midday." River's voice was gravel in a tin.

"I was going to call."

"They always say that. They always say, 'I was gonna call'."

"Aww, poor River, can't get laid."

"I'm too old for that sort of thing."

Red didn't know how old River was. They'd only met three times, and each time she'd judged him a different age. He'd never told her if she was right or wrong. She averaged him at about seventy. Or maybe he'd just had a hard life.

She *knew* he'd had a hard life.

"Tell that to Mick Jagger."

"Huh?"

"He was seventy-three when he had a kid."

"You think I'm seventy-three?"

"Ermmm…"

Three kids, Matty's voice whispered from Nick Strand's head, as it rolled back and forth to the steady movement of the car. She wished she had something she could throw over it. That staring eye.

"So how did it go?" River was on to business now, and his business was caring for her. She hated the word handler. He hated the term father-figure. They'd settled on friend.

"Smooth and by the numbers," she said. "Took the required item."

"You're cleaned up and heading home?"

Red glanced in the mirror again. Blood dried to a dark crust on her cheek and in her eyebrow. A chunk of crispy brain nestled in her ear.

"Pretty much."

River remained silent. He was good at that. Red listened to the wind whispering through the open windows, the wheels humming across hot tarmac, the muttered voice from Strand's severed and mutilated head.

Three kids...why'd you have to...not fair...

The voice was Matty's disbelief and disgust at what she did for a living. He had never known. He'd always believed she was a traveling pharmaceutical rep, making good money selling the newest drugs, and he'd had enough of a problem with that. Matty Van had been a good man—too good for her—and that was why she'd been tearing her soul apart with his voice since the day of his horrible death.

"So?" River asked.

"So...new contract. Came in this morning." She felt the quiver in her voice. River heard it. She knew him so well, she sometimes wondered whether he was also a voice inside her head.

"Red?"

She drove. The sun beat down. Ahead, deeper into the desert, the road floated above the road, a mirage offering her an alternative route. The offer was always there. But her way was set.

"Razor Bill McClintock."

Even above the rumble of the car and the wind through the windows, she heard River's indrawn breath. It was static on the line. It was a punch to the gut.

"Red..."

"You can't talk me out of it."

"Do I ever try? Could I ever?"

"No. And no."

"You took this face to face?"

Red liked to look an employer in the eyes when they asked for someone to die. River had taught her that. Windows to the soul, and all that, but it was true, you could read someone by their eyes. Gauge their seriousness, and sometimes their true purpose.

This one had felt too important.

"Not really," she said. "Video call," she lied. River did not reply. Speaking to someone over a phone was nowhere near the same. You couldn't pick up on body language, atmosphere. Scent.

"Who issued the contract?"

"Alexa Queen. You know her?"

"I know of her."

A pause. She thought she'd lost him, a bad connection maybe. She was heading out into the middle of nowhere.

"And?"

"And that's all. I know of her. Rich through inherited wealth. Plenty of property interests on the west coast. Some shady dealings in Vegas, and when she needs something done, she's very circumspect. Pays well."

"Huh."

"Yeah. Huh. It's not about the money, is it, Red? Did she say why she wanted it done?"

"She said it was personal."

"Yeah, sure, and that's what makes this dangerous. It's personal."

"Of course it is," she said. She wasn't sure she'd actually spoken it aloud, and when Strand said, *It felt personal when you took my fucking head!* that made her even less certain.

"You need to prepare for something like this," River said. "New vehicle, new gear, let yourself settle so that—"

"I've been preparing for seven years," Red said. Her voice was as hot and abrasive as the desert wind through the window.

Strand said nothing. River said nothing.

"Ever since that motherfucker Razor Bill slit Matty's throat, I've been preparing."

"Listen," River said, and he paused, as if working out how to say what he had to say. "Listen, Red—"

"I'm heading into the desert. The place is called Spring Gardens, an old hotel complex that was never finished. I've looked it up, checked it out. Razor is lying low there after a job, thinks he's clean and clear. It'll be easy."

"You've been looking for him for years," River said. "What makes you think it'll be easy?"

"I'll call you when it's done." Red disconnected, then turned her phone off. Cut herself off from River and the outside world. Now it was just her, the car, the shimmering road ahead, and Razor Bill waiting for her bullet in his head.

And me, Strand said. *Don't forget me. The poor bastard you just murdered.*

"Yeah, and you," Dead Red said, and her throat tightened at the sound of Matty's voice in her memory.

Soon, soon, maybe he'd fall silent forever and be at peace, and put her at peace at last.

They called her Dead Red Virgilio because she was dead behind the eyes. She'd died that day back in Boise, Idaho, when she'd returned to her hotel room to find Matty murdered on their bed. His throat was sliced so deeply, his head pulled back so that he could bleed out, that she could see his spine. His eyes were open. On Matty's chest was Razor Bill's calling card—four slashes from a razor, two vertical, two horizontal, and a single small cross in one corner. A never-ending game of tic-tac-toe, a game that would never be won or lost.

Red knew that the murder meant nothing to Razor Bill. A passing death, casual revenge for her taking on a contract he'd also been offered and beating him to the kill. It meant everything to her.

Matty Van had meant everything to her.

Killing Razor Bill would never bring Matty back, but it might return the life to her eyes. And if it didn't save her, at least it would be sweet revenge.

The tall black man parks his truck two miles from the desert building site and walks the rest of the way. He's quiet, careful, moves like a cat. He carries a short sword in a scabbard on his left thigh, and a Dan Wesson DWX pistol in a clip holster on his other hip. He follows the lie of the land, careful not to startle birds aloft or cause dust to rise and drift on the gentle breeze. He's approaching from downwind so the breeze doesn't carry his scent to anyone on the hotel site. He's used to moving like this. He makes himself invisible.

The short white man watches him come. He's been waiting, hunkered down beside a crumbling pallet of building blocks. Once they were destined for walls within which people might live, laugh, fight, make love, but the hotel build was abandoned five years before, and now the blocks have fallen victim to the elements. By night the desert is cold, and sometimes a sheen of frost silvers the grey concrete. Come morning, the sun rises and the temperatures soar, the frost melts, and the concrete slowly, over years, comes apart.

The white man has hardly moved for over five hours. When he needed to piss, he pulled his shorts aside and let it run down his leg. He doesn't mind. Piss dries.

When he sees movement, he resists the urge to hunker down more. He knows how to not be seen. He watches the tall man approach along a low gulley in the land. The tall man is more cautious now, and he's holding the pistol in his right hand.

Moving for the first time in hours, the waiting man lifts the small metal crossbow he's kept hidden in the shadow cast by the pile of blocks, aims, and fires. All in one movement. He flows.

At the last second the tall man senses movement and looks his way, just in time for the bolt to smack home though his left eye. Its entry is smooth, the target soft, and from this close the impact is enough to smash an exit wound through the back of his skull. He's dead before he hits the ground, bone and blood and brains casting a fernlike pattern in the dust behind him.

The short man reloads and remains crouched, still and silent. He breathes through his mouth so that he can hear better. He's waiting for anyone else to come, but knows it's unlikely. The Welshman always works alone.

Thirty minutes later, before he drags the body across to softer ground where he'll bury it in a shallow grave, he takes the razor from his pocket and leaves his mark.

"So you make a cynical profit out of other people's illnesses," Matty Van says. He glances at her sidelong, and Red doesn't know whether or not he's joking. If he isn't joking, then it's a pretty fucking harsh comment from someone she's only just met.

"I make good and fair deals for sought-after medicines so that private providers can help those in need." Red lifts her Old Fashioned and holds it up to him. "Skol."

Matty laughs and clinks her glass with his beer bottle. He sips, still holding her gaze, and a dribble of beer leaks from the corner of his mouth. He wipes it away, not at all embarrassed.

"Another?" he asks, nodding at her glass.

"Shouldn't you stay sober for what you're going to do?"

"I'm much better with a few beers inside me." Matty raises a hand and the barman nods, pouring their drinks without asking what they want.

The Brooklyn bar is thrumming for a sultry Wednesday evening, filled with all manner of people in all types of dress, from torn jeans and band tee-shirts, to swish business suits, to three flamboyant drag artists. They are already orbiting the dance floor, eagerly waiting for the music to begin.

"So you're in the city for work?" Matty asks. Red feels something slip inside her, a flush of coolness flowing through her veins and bones.

"Work, yeah."

Hidden beneath a fold of carpet in the room she's renting is a photograph and a file, and at dawn she'll be collecting a weapon from one of her trusted sources on the East side. By this time tomorrow, her work in the city will be over. If she's planned it right, drug dealing and abusive doctor Gerald Palmer's body will not be found in his apartment for at least three days. And she always plans it right.

"Gotta work tomorrow?" He tips his beer bottle.

Red takes a sip from her drink, using the moment to really look at Matty. His eyes, his smile. His body language. She sees nothing to indicate that he knows her or her work. She's chosen this place at random,

20

and he was already sitting at the bar when she arrived, chatting to the barman. A barfly, maybe. One with attractive wings.

"If I don't have too many of these," she says, laughing. Yes, she is working tomorrow.

"So you've got a suitcase full of drugs?"

"It doesn't work like that."

"So what sort of deals do you do? I mean, few thousand dollars?"

"Try a few million. Pharma is big."

"Big pharma is big!" Matty says, and he chuckles.

I like him, Red thinks, and she takes another sip to try and drown that out. Getting hit on in a Brooklyn bar isn't something she planned, but it's something she can deal with. Drink up, smile, go home.

Except that night, she doesn't. That night, she wonders who is doing the hitting.

"Matty, you're up!" the barman says.

Matty takes a battered hip flask from his pocket, twists off the lid and glugs down a long, deep swig. Red notices it has the word "Van" engraved and painted red on the outside, some of the paint chipped away from frequent use.

"They don't mind you drinking your own stuff in here?" she asks.

"Just my little bit of magic." Matty lifts the flask

to her in a toast, then screws the lid back on and pops it into his pocket. He offers her his fist. They bump, and he goes up onto the small stage and picks up his acoustic guitar.

He plays it like an absolute champ, and dedicates a song to Red, and within an hour she is up dancing with the drag artists and some students and three women who say they are in the Big Apple on a hen week, and who keep calling her Reddy-Red-Red and laughing more every time they do so.

At the end of the night, Matty asks for her number and kisses the back of her hand, staying with her until her Uber shows up.

Nine hours later, she garrots Gerald Palmer and leaves his body folded in a suitcase and wrapped in several soiled blankets in his six-million-dollar condo. She doesn't even need to use the gun. And she doesn't have a hangover.

Four hours after fulfilling her contract, she gets a call from Matty. An hour later, they are walking across Brooklyn Bridge, chatting, laughing, getting to know each other in this impersonal city that she came to intending to leave alone. He is infectious—his quirky sense of humor, his *niceness*. She bathes in his goodness and innocence, and tries to believe it is her own.

That night, they sleep together in Matty's place, and after years of fucking an occasional guy or woman while she was on the road traveling, working, being alone, this time feels like making love.

You always did lie to him, Strand said from the footwell. Red blinked, veering across the road. Damn it, she'd been gone there. Stupid. Most uncool. She was tired, River was right. She should take a rest.

"I never lied to him," Red said. To herself. To Matty's voice coming from the mutilated head. A fly buzzed it. Laying eggs, probably. Let maggots take their fill of what was left of Nick Strand's corrupt mind.

Yeah, right, "I sell drugs."

Red ignored the voice. It whispered and muttered some more, then fell silent. But she sensed it there. The memory of Matty, her conjuring of his sweet innocent soul to challenge and counter all the terrible things she'd done and would yet do.

I did nothing bad to you, my sweet, she thought, and her eyes filled with tears. There was one memory that always came to her in such moments, and she didn't know why it was this one. They'd only been together for a few months, and they'd made enough memories for a lifetime, but even that was never enough, never enough. This one was very random—Matty making coffee in a small apartment they'd rented for a week in a little place close to Boston, rosy from the day they'd spent walking in the hills. He turned to look at her, forgot what he was going to say, frowned, then smiled. And that was it. She couldn't remember what happened afterwards. Couldn't recall the rest of that evening. Some memories were like that, instants in a vast sea of moments that go together to make up a life.

This moment stuck with her. Matty with her, but for a second totally within himself, trying to remember what he'd been going to say. That was Matty Van—present, open, unhindered by conscience or guilt.

You're the guilty one, the voice says. *Take a look at me. If my kids could see me now.*

"Your kids are far better off without you," Red said.

Sure, sure, Dead Red Virgilio, the indisputable compass of morality.

She glanced at her phone. The SatNav showed that she was just a couple of miles from Spring Gardens. She rolled to a stop by the side of the road, got out and stretched. Her back crackled. Her neck popped. She was only in her late-thirties, but she'd lived a life. The running, the hiding, the waiting crouched on hilltops or huddled away in darkened rooms. The occasional fights. She'd smashed her hip in a car wreck in Amarillo. A bullet had shattered her third and fourth ribs on her right side in San Antonio. A knife fight in Cleveland resulted in a punctured lung and broken collar bone. Even so, she kept herself fit and healthy, used the best gyms when she settled down for a few months at a time. The money she made meant she could afford that. She deserved it. She was good at her job, and she only ever killed bad people.

Ha, right, fewer people than if you really had been a big pharma rep, the voice said. Sarcasm, now. She checked there was no one around and walked from the road, looking for somewhere to take a leak.

As she hunkered down, she thought about what was to come. Razor Bill was lying low after a hit, and though he'd be alert and careful, her information suggested he had no reason to suspect any visitors. Alexa Queen had said he was still recovering from a wound picked up a year before. Nerve damage in his left hand. That meant nothing, but she kept it in mind.

It was mid-afternoon. If she was wise, she'd wait until dusk. Razor Bill would be relaxed from the warm afternoon, and not yet alert to dangers from the dark. She *was* wise. But she was also eager.

She finished peeing, blinked, and saw Matty on that bed, his open throat grinning at her, tic-tac-toe on his chest, white sheets red with his good, pure blood.

She stood and returned to the car.

You should let him go, the voice said. The fly had landed on Strand's open left eye. It skittered across the clouded eyeball, pausing to explore his half-closed lid and clean its wings. Mindless to where it stood, ignorant of what those eyes had seen but saw no more.

"I'm not letting him go," Red said. She wasn't sure what the voice meant. Matty saying that killing would bring no peace? Or was it her?

Sometimes, she thought her hatred of Razor Bill was what drove her forward, forward. A part of her had wanted to stop and join Matty when he'd died. One time, a few weeks later and half a bottle of whiskey down, she'd sat on a beach with the warm barrel of a gun stroking the fine hairs of her upper lip. A bullet through the nose, into the brain. Easy way out.

She didn't believe in an afterlife. She hadn't really thought she'd be joining Matty, seeing him again in some cloudy sunlit upland of eternity. All the more reason to end being here without him.

A seagull had changed her mind. It circled above, then dropped a crab onto some rocks nearby to break its shell and get to the tasty morsels inside. She'd heard Matty saying, *Will you look at that?* with his familiar enthusiasm and amazement at nature's many varied and wonderful ways. He'd retained some of the sense of wonder with which kids viewed the world, and it was infectious. Once, the two of them had crouched over an ants' nest and watched their comings and goings for half an hour, brushing ants from their shoes and lower legs, finding amazement in the smallest of things.

Red looked around and saw a lizard scamper across the road, a bird circling overhead, bees buzzing a flowering bush away from the road. She didn't know the names of these animals, and knew Matty probably would have. Seeing them, noticing them, was enough.

"Will you look at that," she said, and she knew that she was going to kill Razor Bill before the sun touched the horizon. Today was a day for wonders.

Back at the car she checked her gun, tucked two spare magazines into her pocket, and slipped her small pocketknife into her belt. If this went to plan, she'd kill him with one bullet, but it was best to prepare for other eventualities. Plans had a way of becoming fluid, like solid ground in an earthquake.

What do you think about when you plan to take a life? the voice said from the passenger footwell.

"Shut up." She sighed, and he kept on talking, Matty's voice muttering in the heat, flowing like a haze above the road. She shut out the words and their meaning, and just listened to the cadence of his voice.

She was glad she could still remember that. Even imagined, even berating her for what she was and what she had done, its timbre and tone brought back some of what she'd loved about him.

Red locked the car door and used a small pencil-sized telescope to scan the land around her. Then she set off for Spring Gardens to kill the man who had murdered her life.

The woman is thin, barely five feet tall, and an old college boyfriend once told her she looks like a nun. It's an appearance she has cultivated. It makes people trust her, and some people barely see her at all. That helps in her chosen career.

Razor Bill McClintock knows The Nun of old. The advantage she has over him here is that he has no idea that she's coming.

The Nun feels a twinge of sadness at the idea of killing Bill. They had a thing together, two decades and a dozen lifetimes ago, and he even said that he loved her. She hadn't loved him. He was a good fuck and fun to be around, but The Nun was very particular about the people she loved. Her father, dead almost thirty years. Yeah, and that was about it.

"Poor Bill," she whispers as she crawls along the unfinished drainage pipe. The words echo a little, like voices whispering back to her in the dark. She hasn't seen Bill in fifteen years. She wonders what he'll look like now, and soon, with her knife in his face. "Poor Bill," she says again, but she doesn't mean it one little bit. A million is a decent amount for such an easy contract. And one less of *them* means more work for *her*. Hell, she'd have killed him for free.

The pipe is barely big enough even for her to winnow her way through, and that's why she chose it. There are spiders, of course. A few scorpions. Twenty meters back, a snake. The Nun carries a blade in one hand to deal with these, and in her other hand, a small penlight. Not too bright, not so that anyone watching might see shadows dancing at the pipe's open end within the hotel complex. Just enough to see. She's found a good rhythm, hips and shoulders shifting and shoving. She'll be there soon.

The short man, razor closed and tucked into his belt, watches the open end of the drainage pipe down in the unfinished trench. They dug out a large pit but never even started building the manhole, and the pipe ends in the open, its mouth drifted with windblown sand. It's dark in there…but not as dark as before. A soft light flickers, shifting back and forth. He can't hear movement yet, but he will. He opens his mouth so that he can hear better. There…a shuffle, a scrape.

He steps down onto the pipe's curved surface, careful to ensure that his shadow is cast away from the opening and no grit or sand slips down. Careful, always careful. He carries a pickaxe that he found in one of the metal storage units the builders left behind. He suspects they had always intended returning to complete the build, but something prevented them from doing so. He holds nothing but scorn for them. Bill has never left a job unfinished.

He hears a soft sigh. Looking down, he sees a pale hand push away some of the sand and soil that has built up in the pipe's mouth. Another sigh as she pushes again. It takes him back, that sound. Making love with her in the back of his truck, her sighs against his ear, telling her that he loved her and never hearing it back.

A job unfinished.

The Nun pulls herself from the pipe, and at the last moment she senses something wrong. Maybe it's a smell, or a sixth sense of someone above and behind her, looking down. She starts to turn, hips and shoulders straining against the pipe, and she readies to lash out with the knife.

Just as she sees Razor Bill standing above her, the

pickaxe comes down into her face. She doesn't even have time to say his name.

Dead Red Virgilio knew more about how Razor Bill worked than Razor Bill himself. She'd made it her mission to do so. Most of the time, she thought it was self-torture, studying everything there was to know about the man who had killed the love of her life. But also, it was research.

Research made her strong.

River told her that, just before the first job they did together. That was the first of the three times they met, sat on the windy Brooklyn waterfront with snow in the air and just a few hardy runners and dog walkers for company. No one considered them odd, sitting in the bad weather and looking across the East River at a Manhattan skyline that would soon be changed forever. This was New York, after all. If they'd been naked and wearing clown masks, maybe people would have looked twice.

Besides, Red and River both had a talent for blending in.

He had a file to give her, he said, but also some advice. "It's not about what's in the file. Never is. Sure, that's the name and the face, the location of the job, other relevant info. But it's just facts. Numbers and names, places and times. It's not the truth. You gotta research to find the truth."

Red asked what he meant.

"Find out what TV channels the target watches. The car they drive. The food they eat when they get takeout. Where they like to walk, eat and drink. The type of deodorant they use, what books they read, whether they prefer giving or receiving head." He paused, looking out across the river. "Or both."

"Why bother with all that?" Red asked. She was still young, with much to learn. "When I'm just going to end up—"

"Shhhhh," River said.

"There's no one around."

"How'd you know?" River didn't seem troubled. He didn't scan around them. He just sat there, the wind lifting his long hair and plucking at his open coat. "Maybe someone's researching me, or you, right now."

Over the years, she'd learned how right he was. She would be given a name and location, but really finding out about her targets always gave her an edge. It had saved her life more than once. Tracking a target in Cleveland and learning she was left-handed meant the knife she came at Red with buried itself in her lung, not her heart.

Razor Bill was a special case. She'd been looking for him for years, and once or twice, she'd come close. All that time searching, closing in, and missing him had taught her a lot about his style and methods. Even learning that he had no real preference for how he killed people was part of that education. The looser he was with his methods, the less particular his habits and preparations might be.

Lying in long, dry grass atop a mound of debris excavated by the hotel building work years ago, Red stared at the unfinished complex. She was looking for movement, but she was also searching for stillness. Razor Bill was known for his patience. It was said that he'd once sat beneath a target's garden hedge for almost thirteen hours waiting for her to return home. Rumor had it he didn't even blink. Bullshit, of course, but it all fed the myth of Razor Bill McClintock.

Red looked back and forth, sometimes with the mini telescope, sometimes without. A few birds took off. She watched them fly, then focussed on where they had roosted. The straight edge of a partially built wall. The level base of a concrete footing. No curves, no natural shapes of someone hiding, waiting, doing the same thing as her.

She blinked sweat from her eyes. Razor liked the high ground, so if he was staying here after a job to let the dust settle, he'd likely have established himself in one of the second-floor spaces. He wasn't a man who went for high-tech very much, but he might have set tripwires or other warning systems. She'd been here an hour and had seen and heard nothing. Soon, it would be time to move.

My bullet in the bastard's head, she thought. A flutter of excitement hit her, and she frowned. Butterflies in her stomach. She never had that. She was focussed, calm, her heart rate only rising if something went wrong with a plan, or if she became involved in an unexpected confrontation. Even then her senses were sharp and attuned to the moment, not edging forward into the near future.

She decided to wait a little while longer before moving in. It wouldn't do to not be totally in control, and she couldn't let anticipation about killing Razor cloud her judgement. *This is just another job*, she thought. *Alexa Queen's paying me to provide a service, and I will provide.*

She saw Matty in their hotel bedroom, dead eyes staring as she came in the door, throat gaping like a second mouth given a long, silent scream.

Red closed her eyes, breathed deeply, and heard

the birds calling from her left. She frowned. Had she missed that? She didn't think so, but with her eyes closed, perhaps she allowed her other sense more clarity.

She looked to the left without moving her head. The spoil heap from the hotel construction continued in that direction, now mostly absorbed back into the land with grasses and low shrubs growing across it, even a few trees in places. Close to the foot of one of these trees, three large rooks were digging in the ground. Pecking at something. Fighting each other, though even from this distance Red could see there was plenty there for them all.

The sudden fear hit her that someone had beaten her to it, and that Razor Bill was no more. *Only at my hand*, she thought, and she felt that fiercely, a powerful need to pull the trigger, plunge the knife. If he was dead and gone then so was her route back to the world.

Revenge. River had always told her it was a dangerous word because it stripped away the purity of what she did. *You're a stone-cold killer*, he said to her the second time they met, and she'd taken no offence. He'd meant it as a compliment. *But revenge, that's hot. And its heat will blind your senses, boil your brain, and make you careless. Revenge never ends well.*

By then, River had a prosthetic leg and one lung

and a metal plate in his skull, and he never slept more than two hours each night because of the pain. He was a walking illustration of every wisdom he shared. He had earned his pain.

Red went low and fast, skirting down the back of the spoil heap and watching the high ground, pistol gripped in one hand. It could be a trap, she knew. Razor didn't usually work like this, but there was no "usual" about Razor. This might just be one more method he was using…set a trap, lure her in, slit her throat and laugh while he did it.

It wasn't a trap. It was The Welshman. The birds saw her coming, stood and watched, and for a second, she thought they'd come at her, too. Then they hopped away to a safe distance, but not too far away from their meal.

He'd been buried face-up. One of his eye sockets was shattered, the misshapen skull displaying the exit wound of whatever had killed him. Not a bullet, she thought. Arrow or crossbow bolt, maybe. Or perhaps Razor had killed The Welshman at close quarters, stabbing him through the face with some sort of spear or other bladed weapon.

Remaining alert for movement or sounds, she knelt beside the shallow grave. The rooks had pecked away his other eye and been working on whatever

was left inside his skull. Red had drunk with him once in Chicago, and he'd told her about how his Welsh heritage made him proud. It was bullshit, she knew, because she'd researched him before their meet. He was as American as they came, born in Detroit to American parents, and his quaint notion of Welshness seemed to be little more than affectation. Still, he had a cool dragon tattoo on his left bicep, and he'd taken great delight in being able to recite that crazy-ass Welsh placename with more letters than a death-row killer's fan base.

"Llanfairpwllgwyngyllgogerychwyrndrobwllllantysiliogogogoch," he'd said after a couple of drink, giggling. She'd liked that about him. He'd giggled like a kid. She knew that he'd executed a man and wife sex trafficking team in Ogunquit two days before.

"Gogogoch," Red whispered, because that was all she could remember. It was eulogy enough, she supposed.

Max Maximillian knows that this is going to be the easiest payday of his career. He knows for three very good reasons. First, Alexa Queen offered him a cool million to off a weak mad old fuck who'd been asking for a bullet in his head for years. Second, Max has never missed a shot or left a target alive, and he knows that he's the best there is. Third, Razor Bill McClintock is his friend. He isn't stupid enough to assume that this will give him an edge over the prick, but if he uses their friendship right, it will give him the valuable, endless couple of seconds he needs.

He strides towards the half-built hotel, glancing left and right. He has a small pistol on a slider up his sleeve, and he can flip it down and shoot in under a second. He's practised, over and over. He's ready. He's able. He smiles and raises his face to the early morning sun.

"Bill!" he shouts. "It's me! Some fucking asshole has put a contract on you. I've come here to help—"

The ground at his feet crumbles and slips away, and he's falling. Max Maximillian has time to utter a startled, "Ulp!" before he lands upright on one of dozens of sharpened wooden stakes lining the bottom of the pit. He swallows his surprise, then shouts in agony when he looks down and sees the bloody spike protruding from the top of his foot.

He holds out his hands, balancing on his injured foot. Unable to reach the edges of the pit. Leg shaking. Knee juddering. All around him, cruel stakes wait to welcome him down.

Goddamnit! Max thinks. "Bill!" he shouts. "Help me, I'm…" Then realization hits, and for just a few seconds he's one of only two people who understands exactly what is going on.

He hears the scrape of feet on the dusty ground above and behind him.

Bill watches from a distance as Max Maximillian—and what a stupid arrogant fuck he was to call himself that, like some computer game killer—edges towards the hotel's main entrance. When the pit swallows him up and he hears, "Bill, help me, I'm…" he is already walking toward the pit. In one hand, he carries his rifle.

In the other hand, something else.

As he arrives at the pit and Max turns on one precarious, bloody foot to face him, Razor Bill thinks, *All too easy.*

"Catch," he says, and he throws the diamondback at his old friend.

Max yelps, lashes out with both hands to shove the serpent from him, and falls back. Bill hears the *crunch!* of several stakes entering Max's flesh, and then the man begins to scream.

Still nursing the rifle—just in case, he can't be too careful, this has only just begun—he moves to the edge of the pit and looks down.

Max is lying on his side. He must have at least six stakes piercing him, including one though his left wrist, another pinning his right arm beneath him, and one that's sliced into the back of his neck. It holds his head still as the rattler slithers across the pit floor, veering smoothly around the stakes, heading for the screaming man's face.

Razor Bill looks up at the sun. It's going to be a hot one. For a second, he considers climbing down into the pit to leave his mark, but the snake's still down there, and he's pissed it off enough already today. And besides, no one will see it. Instead, he heads around the side of the building, still listening to his old friend's screams, and starts filling a wheelbarrow with sand. When he dumps in the first load, he notices that Max has the snake grasped in his mouth, its head hanging off by a thread. Impressive. He fetches another load and continues filling the hole, Max Maximillian pinned down there like an ugly butterfly, uttering frantic and terrified groans through a mouthful of rattler.

By the time he finishes, it's ninety degrees, and he knows that his other guests will be arriving very soon.

The Welshman being dead changed everything. Red had to assume that Razor Bill killed him. Alexa Queen had contracted more than one resource, possibly as insurance but perhaps for other reasons. Red never assumed the simplest explanation was the most likely.

She took one last look at the dead man, then headed away from the hotel. Razor would know that he was not safe here anymore, and that stole away her element of surprise. He'd killed one, he would be waiting for others, if he was even still here.

If he'd fled, she had lost her chance. But there would be others.

She had to take stock and rethink her approach.

She moved away from Spring Gardens, sometimes taking the low ground, other times skirting across the slopes of small hills and dunes, never predictable, always shifting direction and bearing. If anyone was following, she wanted to confuse them. If anyone was watching—through binoculars, or a scope—she hoped to lose them. Soon she found somewhere she felt safer, a low dune with a shallow and overgrown dip on the top where she could lie out of sight and keep watch over the surrounding landscape.

"Damn it," she whispered, then caught herself. She shouldn't be talking. Probably shouldn't even be moving. *Everything you've learned, here and now,* she thought, and she slipped her phone from her pocket with one hand, still grasping her pistol in the other. She had to expect Razor Bill to find and attack her at any moment.

He's gone, she thought, but she shook that idea, tried to lay it to rest. She didn't know him, but she knew *about* him. He liked what he did. He liked tic-tac-toe. She thought it more likely that once he'd confronted and killed The Welshman, he'd stay to take on whoever else might be part of the contract.

Maybe now she could find out who those others might be.

Constantly alert to movement or sound or shifting scent around her, she accessed an app on her phone and waited for the map to load. Even River didn't know about this, as evidenced by his name being at the top of the short list revealed on the screen. Below him were The Welshman, Amanda Boom and Song For Lemmy, names all in bold blue. In black, Razor Bill McClintock and several others who she suspected weren't even operative anymore. These were the ones she'd not been able to implant with a tracking pod, but she maintained their names. River always said she should live in hope.

Instead of touching each name, she used her

thumb and forefinger to swipe and reduce the map to the several square miles around Spring Gardens. The Welshman was the first pulsing circle to appear, less than half a mile from where the map placed her right now. She remembered the concert where she'd stuck him, sweaty and gyrating bodies pressed close in a dark, hot room, music pounding from the stage and rattling her heart in her chest, and The Welshman leaning into a tall man who was his companion for the night. The last song of the gig, the frenetic jumping and singing, and she'd pushed through bodies and reached out, pricking the thinnest needle into his right buttock. He hadn't even felt it, and she'd left before the song was done. Beat the rush.

Now his circle was unmoving, and it would never move again. She looked at it for a while, and then another circle flickered to life less than a mile to the east. Amanda Boom.

"Amanda," Red whispered. They'd had a drunken night out in Seattle four years before. Sitting outside a bar on the waterfront, constantly checking that there were no people close enough to hear, Red talked about Matty Van's death, without revealing she knew who'd killed him. Amanda had met him once and was sad on her behalf. They considered each other good friends, though they'd only met a handful of times. Sometimes, reputation was enough to get to know somebody. Similarity of experience. This was their ninth meeting, and earlier Amanda had said they should slit thumbs and become blood sisters. That night was the first time Red had told anyone other than River the reasons why she'd become what she was—her mother left when she was young, her father did his best, she helped him where she could, until he got mixed up with bad people and ended up with his pockets filled with rocks in a Michigan lake. Ever since, Red had hated bad people. She'd figured she might as well monetize her hate. Her first kill—the guy who'd paid to have her father trussed up and drowned—she'd done for free.

The intensity of that evening was supercharged with the knowledge of what she and Amanda did. The secrets they hid. After another bottle of wine, they'd compared their most successful hits. Red went first, recounting the cool million she'd received for offing a corrupt businessman who was renowned for beating his kids. His wife had paid the money, with thanks. Amanda had nodded, impressed, then rattled off three names. When Red frowned, she told her they used to run one of the largest child abuse sites on the dark net. She'd received a hundred thousand dollars combined for all three hits.

That was how Amanda judged success. Red had fist-bumped her, ordered more booze, and at the end of the night she'd bundled Amanda into an Uber, holding her face and kissing her on each cheek while she pricked a needle into her left earlobe. Red had departed their unusual, probably dangerous evening liking Amanda Boom more than ever.

She wondered how Amanda might rank killing Razor Bill on her table of success.

She also wondered whether Alexa Queen had offered them all the same fee.

He's mine, she thought, following the slow-moving circle. *You just leave him alone.*

As she went to reduce the map to see where in the country Song For Lemmy might be—she'd stuck him in the thigh on a train station platform two years ago, ducking away through an exit door as Song rubbed his leg and looked around, frowning—his circle also appeared. Of course it did. As River had once told her, when things started to go south, get ready for Antarctic cold.

Song's circle was far closer than she would have liked. So close that she pressed herself flatter to the ground, slowing and softening her breath. Held the gun before her, resting on her other hand.

Fuck, this was getting complicated. She considered

49

her options, then choice was taken from her as a gunshot sang out. Soil and grit blasted up close to her face and she rolled, powering herself out of the hollow and down the slope's side facing away from Spring Gardens. Another shot plucked at her right sleeve as she went, nicking her wrist, and she slid down the slope and pressed herself flat to the ground.

The shots and impacts were almost instantaneous. Whoever was shooting at her was close, but she didn't think it had been Amanda or Song. This was Razor Bill, come to harvest the assassins sent to take him down.

From her right she heard three cracks from a different weapon, so close together that they echoed as one. Then rapid footsteps. She pointed her own gun in that direction, and a shape dashed along a shallow gulley, crouched down. Amanda Boom. Her hair was black now, not blond, and she looked sleek and fit. She skidded to a halt when she saw Red and crouched down, hands held up and out.

Red lowered the gun. Interesting. Amanda didn't seem surprised to see her there.

"See him?" Red asked.

"A glimpse. Behind the rusted excavator."

"A glimpse!" a voice called out, and Rec recognised Razor Bill McClintock. She had to fight against every instinct she had to jump up and run at him, blasting bullets into his face. That's what he wanted. Two seconds after standing her brains would be dripping down her back.

Amanda crawled closer to her and Red pointed her gun.

"Hey, no worries from me," Amanda whispered. "What the fuck's going on? I just found The Nun in a ditch with a pickaxe in her face!"

"The Nun?" Red had heard of her, but never met her. She did most of her work in South America, and most of the rest of them lumped her in with a loose group of contract killers they called the Tickers. Because their life clocks were ticking down. Careless, throwing caution to the wind, they went from job to job just waiting for the bullet with their name on to catch them up. It looked like The Nun had been caught. By a pickaxe, not a bullet, but still. Tick...tick...silence.

"What do you think—" Amanda began, but another shot took her voice and they both flinched and scanned their surroundings. Red didn't trust Amanda—none of them trusted anyone, that was the way of it, that's why those of them who were still alive were still alive, but...

"Who contracted you?" Red asked, but she thought she already knew.

"Dead Red Virgilio! The fuck you doing here?"
Song For Lemmy appeared behind her, snaking
his way along the gulley—as effectively as a two-
hundred-and-thirty-pound chunk of muscle and bad
deeds could snake—with a classic revolver in each
hand, mother-of-pearl handles worn smooth with
use. He wore a cowboy hat and white boots, just like
his rock-star namesake and hero. She'd never heard
him singing.

"Being herded, hunted down and killed, by the
looks of things," Red said.

"Huh?"

"Dead Red Virgilio! The fuck you doing here?"
Razor called out, and his voice shook with laughter.
She saw him kneeling on Matty's back and gripping his
hair, other hand tugging a knife hard across his throat,
and she wondered if he'd been laughing then, too.

Red half-crouched and let off three shots towards
the old excavator fifty meters away. Two of them
ricocheted from the metal. Razor laughed from
somewhere else.

Song grabbed her shoulder and pulled her down.
"Huh?" he asked again. He'd never been renowned for
being the brightest spark in the campfire, but he had a
smooth instinct for killing and, more importantly, not
being killed. Many had tried. One more was trying now.

"Dead Red Virgilio," Razor called again, "and Amanda Boom, and Song For Lemmy, and poor old…" He laughed, and his voice broke, then rose. "Poor old Welshman."

"Oh shit," Red said.

"That sounds just like…"

"You never should have listened to Alexa Queen," Razor said, his voice high and light. His voice that of Alexa Queen. A second later, Red heard a low, dull *whump!*

She stood and ran, away from the small hill and the two other killers and the unfinished hotel beyond, but in that moment she knew that it really didn't matter which way she fled. The grenade would fall where it fell.

Red is still a little breathless. Killing Strand was easy, but cutting off his head raised her sweat. Part of that was effort; most of it was in her own goddamn skull. Her thoughts. Imagining the knife in another person's hand, a different head on kinder shoulders. When his head flopped off and hit the floor, she nudged it with her foot so that Mike Strand was looking up at her. She had to make sure it wasn't Matty Van.

53

TIM LEBBON

Still sweating, pleased with a job well done, she jumps as her phone chimes. It's a particular ringtone for a separate line installed on her phone, the sound of a sanctioned job coming in, usually through River but sometimes through a wider agency. She wasn't expecting anything quite so soon.

She answers in her usual way. With silence. River taught her that; make them uncomfortable, make them talk, and they'll spill more than they intended.

A few seconds pass.

"Er, is that Red Virgilio?"

"Uh-huh."

"My name is Alexa Queen. I hope you don't mind me calling you cold like this."

*You're even colder than I thought…*Mike Strand's lifeless head says, and Red sighs. *Hello Matty*, she thinks. *You didn't take long this time.* He's lived dead inside her head for every second since she found him on that bed. He was so alive in her imagination before that, a sculpture of love slowly, slowly constructing itself on a pedestal she'd always sworn would never be filled. She could not afford love. There was no place in her life for it. But with Matty, love gave her no choice.

"No problem," she says.

"I have a position that needs filling, and you are the ideal candidate."

54

"Uh-huh." Red always finds this fake talk amusing. Positions and commissions, painting jobs, bulk-buys…just tell me who the fuck you want me to kill.

"The position is currently occupied by someone, but he's just not working out. I'm afraid I'm going to have to let him go." Alexa Queen sounds posh. Rich. Probably sitting behind an oak desk with just a phone and nothing else marring the surface. Or by a pool somewhere, a muscled guy half her age sun-creaming her back. Or maybe sipping a cocktail. Whatever.

"How did you get this number?" Red asks.

"Oh, I assure you I went through all the right channels," Alexa Queen says. "I'm aware that your number isn't listed, but—"

"There's a green-code button beside the steering wheel," Red says.

"Oh…er…push it and you'll get zero to sixty in two-point-eight."

Red remains silent. So does Alexa, for a while. Tough to rattle.

"That's…right?"

"What's the position? And who currently occupies it?"

"The position is head of marketing for a small but very exclusive west-coast fashion dealership.

The current post holder is a man named William McClintock."

Red's gut drops. A chill goes through her. Hearing that name from another mouth is strange, almost surreal, because since Matty's murder, McClintock has been so much a part of her. Every breath she takes she considers his death. Between blinks, she thinks of the ways she will kill him. She's looked, but he proves elusive. He's a master of going to ground, emerging only to fulfil a job before vanishing again like a bad dream. Even River, with his contacts and reach, barely hears whispers about Razor Bill.

"Did you hear?"

"Uh-huh."

"I'm offering a competitive commission plan. Seven figures over a year. Is that acceptable?"

Red nods, and Mike Strand's lifeless eyes watch her. He says nothing. Maybe even Matty, good man though he was, would approve of her avenging his brutal murder.

"With benefits," Red whispers, and Alexa says something else, piffle to disguise what this call is really about, but Red doesn't hear a word.

She sees Razor Bill killing her Matty Van, and everything else goes away.

The explosion thumped the ground behind her and slammed into her ears, driving scoring sand against the back of her neck and bare arms, shoving her forward. She kept her footing and zigged-zagged, scampering across an old, rutted track and skidding on her side into the ditch beyond. Another *whump!* of a grenade launching, and this time the explosion was further away.

"Benefits!" Razor Bill screeched in Alexa Queen's voice, and Red had to admire the bastard's balls. Being confident enough to fool them all with a made-up voice took nuts the size of Godzilla's.

She was going to cut them off.

She checked her gun, ran her hands across the back of her head and other places where she hurt—a smear of blood, but she wasn't badly injured—then tensed, readying herself. He'd expect them to be running and trying to hide, and that made this the perfect time to go on the offensive.

Red stood to run toward where she thought Razor Bill was hiding.

A bullet skimmed her left cheek, accompanied by the blast of the gunshot. She fell to her right, back into the ditch. She crawled rapidly, scuffing her knees and elbows, and went to stand again.

Three shots rang out, the same as she'd heard before. Amanda Boom. A bullet struck metal. Two more hissed past close by. Someone shouted. She heard the familiar *slip-click* of a pistol having a new magazine inserted. Footsteps whispered through loose sand.

Red stood again and fired three times, spreading her aim back the way she'd come, hoping to keep Razor down. She took a few more steps—

A bullet hit her right thigh, ripping right through. She fell again and rolled onto her left side, hand clamped to the wound, mouth shut tight. She didn't want to give Bill the pleasure of hearing her cry out. She felt the warmth of blood against her hand, the ice-heat of pain readying to scorch through the shock. She looked down, lifted her hand a little. The wound was bleeding, but not too much. Not the artery, at least she didn't think so.

Fuck!

"Red?" Amanda called. She appeared along the ditch and closed the distance between them. "You okay?"

"I got shot."

"And?" Amanda scanned Red's body, crawling close so that her face was inches from the wound. "Looks fine. Straight through the fatty bit, missed the artery. Just another scar, right?"

Red frowned, then remembered. Drunk on that Seattle waterfront, they'd flowed into their own version of that crazy scene from *Jaws*, comparing scars until Red said they were attracting too much attention, and Amanda had said, well, pity, I was just going to show you when I got shot through my right ass cheek.

"Just another scar," Red said. She used her pocketknife to slice off the leg of her trousers beneath the knee, then tied it tightly around the wound. Wincing, she said, "Where is he?"

"Higher ground. Got us pinned down. Oh hey, here's Song."

Song loped across the ground beyond the ditch, crouched so low that his knees almost met his face as he ran. He had both guns raised. Red just waited for the bullet that would blast that stupid hat from his scalp. It didn't come. He leapt into the ditch.

"He's running," he said. "Saw him heading back to the hotel. Half a hotel. Whatever."

"So what now?" Amanda asked.

Red was shaking. The pain, yeah, but the fury, too. The hatred she felt for this man who had killed her lover and then played her, employing her to come and kill him so that he could...

"How many others?" Red asked.

TIM LEBBON

"Did he contract, do you mean?" Amanda asked.

"The Welshman," Red said. "And The Nun. Anyone else you know of? Jiggy Jenny, maybe?"

"Caught a headful of lead in San Diego six months back," Amanda said. "Maybe Prince Harming?"

"That idiot," Red said. "Fell thirty-two stories in Toronto. Cracked a perfectly good sidewalk. Max Maximillian?"

"No one's seen anything of him in years," Amanda said. "Rumors he's retired to South America. My guess is he's in an unmarked grave somewhere. Good riddance. Arrogant fuck."

"Ain't so many of us left anymore," Song said. "Not the old guard, at least. New ones coming on the scene, but they're so fucking *gauche*."

Amanda laughed. "Guess the bastard's thinning the herd."

"Then let's thin *him*. Strip by strip." Song holstered one revolver and drew out a huge knife from his trouser leg.

"Where the hell did you hide that?" Amanda gasped.

"That's what all the ladies ask."

"Not appropriate," Red said. "Watch it or you'll get cancelled."

"Been cancelled before," Song said. "Came back."

60

"Well, that motherfucker's trying to cancel us all," Amanda said. "So I say we join forces. Eh?"

"I only work alone," Red said.

"Holy shit, the cliché queen strikes!"

"What about the commission?" Song asked. "We gonna split it?" Not the brightest spark.

"I'm just in this for him," Red said. "He killed the man I love."

"Oh," Amanda said, and she gave Red a strange look.

"What?"

"Personal," Amanda said. "You know I'm sorry about Matty. He was a nice guy. But personal makes it dangerous."

"Personal makes *me* dangerous," Red said. "So, what's the—"

"I got a plan," Song said. He chuckled. "Used this one seven months ago during a job in Chattanooga. Put my shoulder out."

"Is it better now?" Amanda asked.

"It's better."

"So what's the plan?" Red asked. Cautious. Song For Lemmy was a big man and no slouch when it came to killing people for money, but he was also no master strategist. And that was a nice way of putting it. A harsher way would be to say he was thick as

61

TIM LEBBON

pigshit, and had succeeded in his chosen career up to now mainly due to his focus and single-mindedness. Not being an overthinker sometimes paid dividend.

"Tell me where you found The Welshman."

R ed doesn't believe in accidental meetings, and in her line of business they put her on edge. Make her suspicious. It's a healthy outlook, and the day she bumps into Amanda Boom just inside a New York diner she sess a similar reaction reflected in her friend's eyes.

In a matter of seconds, Red scrolls through all the considerations and calculations that will keep her safe. *We chose this place at random, walked back and forth across several streets and blocks, she can't have followed us. She looks as surprised at me, and she's thinking the same things I am. There's a front door, a side entrance, and exit through the kitchen behind the counter. I can draw my Glock in two seconds.*

Then Amanda holds out her hand to Matty and says, "So Red's decided to go for good-looking guys for a change."

Matty actually blushes. He takes her hand, and Amanda pulls him in for a hug. Over his shoulder she pouts at Red, and mouths, *He's hot!*

62

Matty and Amanda part and Red smiles at the other woman. "What're you doing in New York?" Then, a loaded question. "Work?"

"Just a bit of R & R," Amanda says. "You?"

"Same." Red looks around the diner, taking the opportunity to check out the other patrons. It's mid-afternoon and the place is busy, and she looks for anyone she recognises. More importantly, she is alert for furtive glances from anyone who might recognise her.

"Food's great here," Amanda says. She taps her stomach. "Halloumi burger to die for. Join you for a coffee, though, while you order?"

Red smiles and feels some of the tension draining from her shoulders. Only some. She stays wired.

Instinctively, Amanda and Red head for a booth at the back of the diner, close to the kitchens. When Red turns back, Matty is waiting at an empty window booth. He points, shrugs. The view isn't amazing—just a New York street bustling with New York people going about their busy days—but Red knows how Matty likes to people watch. She gestures after Amanda and returns his shrug.

They sit in the booth at the back and drink coffee and chat, and Amanda talks to Matty without pressure, and without anything that approaches interrogation.

She's open and friendly, and Red feels herself relaxing more and more.

It has been over three months since her last job. She is enjoying her time with Matty. She's falling in love.

"I'm jealous," Amanda says.

"Of me?"

"Sure." She glances at Matty. "Of both of you. Having the opportunity to meet someone, spend time, get to know each other past all the usual 'what music do you like, what's your favourite drink, can I touch this hole or that one' banter."

Matty almost snorts coffee. Red laughs, and it feels unforced and healthy.

"Your work doesn't give you that opportunity?" Matty asks.

"I travel a lot," Amanda says. "Never even bothered buying a property. I rent here and there, from time to time, but I'm on the road so much."

"What do you do?"

Red tenses, and she and Amanda swap a glance. They are both still smiling.

"I'm a systems designer, freelance, go into big companies and formulate their computing needs and requirements, establish design parameters. Try to push the envelope, where I can. AI is going to have a really big effect soon."

"Ah'll be back," Matty says in a Schwarzenegger voice.

"Yeah, something like that," Amanda says, and she looks at Matty over her coffee cup.

"Matty and I are heading upstate for a few days," Red says, even though at that moment she knows that she will change their plans. Matty won't like it, but she'll work her ways with him. Replace their trip with something better. She can afford it. He doesn't know she has over six million dollars in a dozen different bank accounts at home and overseas, and he never will. But she enjoys spending her money on him, and on them. And she knows that he enjoys it too. Matty Van grew up poor, and if Red has her way, he'll never feel poor again.

"Sounds nice," Amanda says. "Doing what?"

"Hiking, exploring, travelling around a bit."

"So where's work taking you next?" Matty asks.

"South." Amanda finishes her coffee, and for a moment there's an uncomfortable silence. Red catches her glancing at Matty once or twice, and she's afraid Amanda is going to say more, or spill something that will plant a seed of suspicion in Matty's mind. Naive to her world he might be, but he is also intelligent, and sharp at picking up subtext. She remains fucking amazed that he still believes she's in pharmaceuticals.

"Been lovely seeing you," Red says. "We should do this more often."

"Bump into each other at random?" Amanda stands, stretches, twists a kink out of her back. "Too many hotel beds."

Amanda bids them a fond farewell, gives them both hugs, and walks away. She leaves the diner and only glances at them again through the window as she walks along the sidewalk. Matty raises a hand and waves. Red nods.

"She was nice," Matty says. "How come you've never mentioned her?"

"Haven't I?"

Matty laughs, then signals the waiter to place their food orders. *Haven't I?* is Red's standard response. She feigns having a bad memory, and that smooths over any mistakes she might make in casual conversation, whether overt or through omission.

The next time Red sees Amanda Boom is in Seattle, and Matty is food for worms and bugs.

Red knew that Razor Bill would be on the offensive. They'd discussed that. Song had seen him hurrying back towards the half-finished hotel, and they all knew that was a feint. He'd started with The Welshman and The Nun, and he meant for them all to be dead by the time the sun went down.

Red's leg blazed with pain. She'd necked a strong painkiller, but she didn't want to do anything that dulled her senses or reaction time. The pains inside would always trump the agonies from mere physical wounds, and she used them to drive her, motivate her. Her cheek was bleeding. Her leg felt heavy and hot, but she could still move reasonably well. She knew she didn't have long; the shock would wear off and her leg would soon begin to stiffen and bruise.

In any event, she knew that this would all be over within the hour.

Amanda crouched to her left. To her right, Song readied himself. Two competitors, one who she called a friend, and just like most of the old guard they had always prided themselves on working alone. Teaming up brought its own possibilities of double crosses, and none of them trusted anyone more than themselves.

Red hoped this crazy idea would work. But glancing at Song, she wondered yet again how the fuck he'd talked them into it.

"Ready?" Amanda asked.

"Yeah. Let's give it a go."

Amanda broke left, dashing from cover to cover

and working her way around the north edge of the Spring Gardens site.

With a wink at Song, Red went right. She kept low and moved fast, careful and steady. She'd considered keeping one eye on the tracking app on her phone, fearing what Amanda and Song might do. But she was as convinced as she could be that Razor Bill had played them all, and they'd already seen the results of his scheming.

Hell, right now Red could still smell death in her nostrils.

She kept her phone in her pocket. She could not afford to be distracted.

Pausing behind a pile of roofing joists that had cooked in the sun and become brittle and discoloured, she heard something scampering around in there. Some small mammal or lizard. She kept watch for snakes. There were trails in the dust around her boots.

Her thigh screamed as she crouched down. Inside, she screamed back. She blinked and saw Bill juddering and dancing as she pumped bullets into his chest.

She edged around the side of the pile and scanned the hotel with her pocket telescope. Some of the unfinished window openings had polythene sheeting fixed over them, and much of it had come loose to flap in the gentle breeze. She tried to see inside, but even though the structure had no roof, if was shadowy in there. If Bill could draw them in he'd have them at a disadvantage.

He knew that. He knew that they'd know that. Which was another reason she believed he'd still bring the fight to them.

She dashed from cover, heading for a crooked old storage container that sat rusting into the ground, and gunshots echoed from half-finished walls. She skidded to a halt by the container and turned her head slightly left and right.

Another shot. Amanda.

Red grimaced as she moved, feeling blood filling her shoe, her leg growing heavy, foot dragging. She could fight against the pain forever, but her control over the physical effects of being shot would not last for long.

Gun at the ready, she headed across the site toward the gunfire.

And there was Razor Bill, crouched behind a spoil heap nursing a rifle. He shouldered it and fired back towards the hotel at something she couldn't see, and though she was too far away to get an accurate shot with the pistol, she let off a couple.

Bill flinched, then edged away from the pile of building debris.

Another *crack!*, then she saw Amanda a couple of hundred meters away. She was running, crouching, firing, driving Bill away from the hotel and toward Song. Red joined her, limping badly now, but harassing Bill so that he didn't have time to consolidate his ground and return fire.

With the rifle, he'd pick them off as soon as they gave him the chance. So they didn't. Instead, they herded him, ducking into cover when he paused to aim and shoot, squirming low to the ground and rising again, taking pot shots at him and edging him closer and closer to where Song was waiting.

"I'm not stupid, Dead Red Virgilio!" he shouted. "Not like you! You'll believe anything!"

Red crawled around a stack of metal drums and squeezed off two shots. Razor barely ducked. He laughed and scurried away, disappearing around a low, wide mound of sand.

Red knew what awaited him on the other side. She dashed forward, reloading as she went, and as she reached the top of the pile she saw Razor some distance ahead, standing motionless before a copse of trees.

Emerging from those trees was The Welshman. The man he had shot through the eye with a crossbow bolt. Even from this distance Red could see the damage to The Welshman's head, and close up it must have looked horrific.

Razor Bill, at least half-mad, stood aghast. Somewhere in his damaged mind, he twisted the reality of what he saw. The Welshman was a dead man, a corpse risen for revenge.

His shock and terror only lasted for a few seconds, but it was long enough to allow Song for Lemmy to carry the dead man's corpse—propped by a couple of stiff lengths of wood—close enough to start shooting.

As Bill realised his mistake just as Song opened fire. The range was less than twenty meters, and the first two bullets struck Razor center-mass, sending him staggering and falling onto his back.

Song dropped the corpse and flexed his shoulder, gun still aimed with the other hand.

Red saw Amanda approaching from the right, and she ran down the slope to intercept. She'd told them that Razor was her kill. She'd told them why. But as Song fired two more times, she realised her mistake.

Never trust a killer.

"Don't finish him!" she shouted.

Distracted, Song glanced up, and a bullet from Razor's rifle blasted off his lower jaw and tore open his throat. He stood there for a few seconds, then took three shaky steps backwards before crumbling like a shattered mannequin.

Razor rolled onto his stomach, then up onto all fours. He lifted the rifle with one hand and let off a wild shot, and from the corner of Red's eye she saw Amanda stagger and fall.

"Amanda?"

No reply.

Red fired at Razor as she ran, and as he swung the rifle her way she knew she had seconds to live. Somehow—bullet-proof vest or Kevlar, or just plain luck—Song's bullets hadn't damaged him enough, and with his rifle he was unlikely to miss at this range.

Red was out in the open with no cover.

She skidded to a stop, braced in a shooter's stance, and remembered Matty's breath in her ear as he kissed her, his touch on her arm, and most of all his laugh. Innocent. Naive. Beautiful.

Her bullet flipped Razor's head to the side and he fell, trapping the rifle and the hand that held it beneath him.

Red closed the distance between them, stopping ten meters away. Close enough to put the last bullet into his face, far enough away to twist aside and duck if he'd fallen onto a grenade.

He's fucking mad, she thought. He would do anything to win, even if it meant his own life.

Razor Bill was grunting. She thought he was struggling for breath, perhaps with a bullet in his lung or throat. She took a few steps closer before realising it was laughter.

"Funny?" she asked.

"Funny," he said. He lifted his head to look at her, arm and rifle still trapped beneath him. He didn't try to move, roll, shoot at her again. She thought his shooting days were over. Her bullet had scored along the right side of his head, and she could see his skull beneath the fallen flap of scalp. He hadn't escaped all of Song's bullets, either. His left side was soaked with blood.

"Kevlar?" she asked.

He shook his head and winced. He must have had the mother of all headaches.

"Just a vest. Didn't catch them all."

"I need you to look at me, Bill."

"I am looking at you."

"In the eye. I need you to look me in the eye and tell me...why."

Bill looked her in the eye, a crooked grin filled with pain. He was bleeding a lot. His right eye was flushed with blood, and Red thought his skull and eye socket was probably fractured. He might not have long left.

"Why?" she asked.

"Because…I've always been the best."

"The best?"

"And lately…my confidence has…slipped. And…well, Dead Red Virgilio…I'm thinking about retirement."

"What?" She shook her head. "That's not what I mean."

Razor frowned, then groaned. He changed position a little, and the gun scraped on the gravel.

Red tensed, took a step closer. Three pounds pressure on a five pounds trigger. One twitch from retiring Razor forever.

"I mean, why Matty?"

"Why Matty what?"

"Why kill Matty Van? Why take away the man I…the one I…"

Razor chuckled. It hurt him, so he stopped. "Matty *who*?"

Red blinked. "The man I loved."

"Why would I want to kill some limp dick you hooked up with, Dead Red?"

Matty's throat gaping open. The bed turned red. Tic-Tac-Toe carved into his chest, a cross in one corner. A game begun, a game she was going to end here.

"Because you're mad."

Razor laughed again, through the pain this time. A fly had landed on the bloody wound on his head. His right eye rolled now, crying tears of blood.

From behind, Red heard Amanda Boom approach. Dragging one foot. She glanced back, nodded once at Amanda…then froze.

"He never told you I wanted him," Amanda said. It seemed to make her upset. "If he had, you'd have killed me the moment you—"

She broke off. Her eyes went wide. She went to crouch, an instinctive reaction to reduce her surface area, and lifted her gun.

Even as Red turned to Razor again, she thought, *It might just be a bluff.*

But Razor had rolled onto his bloodied side, and was dragging the rifle out from beneath him, shoving it forward, lifting it one-handed again to blast Red's confusion to pieces.

Red squeezed her trigger and Razor's head snapped back, mouth open wide, and a haze of blood and brains spattered across the ground behind him.

Red spun around just as another shot rang out from Amanda. A fist punched her chest, shoving her back and down. She gripped her gun hard as she struck the ground, rolled, came up into a sitting position as a second bullet kissed her neck—

—Matty kissing her neck, just beneath the ear where she loves it, and he knows everything she loves. He learned it all so quickly, as if hers is a song he has been waiting to sing his whole life—

—and she fired off three quick shots. With her fourth squeeze of the trigger, the gun jammed. Dust. Sand. Bad fucking luck.

Amanda staggered back a few steps, looking down at the spreading bloom of blood on her stomach. She tried to ease herself down onto her knees, but the pain was too much, or maybe her spine had been winged. She fell onto her back.

Red tried to stand. She was winded, could hardly breathe, thought she'd cracked a few ribs, and for a moment she didn't know what had happened. She pulled her tee shirt collar out and looked down, and a bright bruise was already spreading across her chest right above her heart. She delved into her jacket pocket and found Matty's hip flask, bent and dented, with a deformed bullet embedded in its skin. *Just my little bit of magic*, she thought. If Amanda had been using a chunkier caliber, her lungs would have been splattered across Razor Bill's corpse.

She gasped in a shuddering breath at last.

Amanda Boom still gripped her weapon, trying to lift it, resting it on her leg and pointing it at Red, squeezing. The bullet went way wide. Red staggered to Amanda, fell on her, and Amanda screamed in agony. Red grabbed her gun and tugged it from her grasp.

"What?" Red croaked. Then she shouted it, against the pain, filled with fury. "*What? What?*"

Amanda's breath came fast and light. It was hurting her to breathe, and Red pushed herself up so she was straddling the other woman's hips. Amanda had a bullet in her gut and another in her hip. She'd be dead quite soon, but it might take a while. A gutshot was the worst.

"What?" Red asked again. "Amanda?"

"Matty," Amanda said. "You were so happy with him. In love. I was jealous, and he just seemed…"

"Perfect," Red said, and all emotion dropped from her voice.

"Yeah. I asked him…to come to me."

"When?"

Amanda Boom laughed. "He didn't tell you. I thought people in love tell each other everything."

"So you killed him."

Amanda looked to one side. She looked almost ashamed, but Red knew it couldn't be that. Amanda was never ashamed of anything.

No, this wasn't shame. It was regret.

"If I couldn't have him, no one could," Amanda said.

Regret that Matty Van had told her no.

"So you made it look like Razor."

"He's mad. No one would doubt it."

Red breathed deeply, wondering if there was anything else she needed to know. Whether Matty had considered what Amanda was asking. Whether she'd told him anything about what she did for a living. And she wondered what Matty had thought when he was alone in that hotel room and Amanda Boom had appeared at the door.

"Did he let you in?" she asked.

Amanda looked straight at her. "Oh, he wanted me," she said. "His dick got hard the second he saw me. He knows a real woman when he—"

Red shot her in the face. Then again in the heart. Then she stood and shouted, angry at herself for being led, furious with Amanda for having the final say.

She knew I was going to make her hurt, Red thought. *She goaded me into killing her quickly.*

She looked back at the dead woman, then crouched and sat by her side. Her face was a mess, skull ruptured, all those thoughts and histories and stories scattered in the sand. Living to dead in the crack of a skull and the spill of brains.

It always gave Red pause.

She waited for Matty to say something from Amanda Boom's corpse—an accusation, even a thanks for putting him at rest. But there was nothing. Perhaps she'd heard Matty's voice for the last time, except in precious memory.

"I love you," she said, and she cried, because her greatest pain was that she had never told him.

Everyone has secrets that need whispering from time to time.

Red could hardly walk, let alone drag Song For Lemmy's bulk out of the blazing sun. She made do with piling some old building blocks around him, making some sort of temporary mausoleum. The animals would still get in, the stench of rot would escape. She didn't know any Motörhead lyrics, so she said, "Rock on, Song," and left him to his rest.

She used her pocketknife to carve a tic-tac-toe in Razor Bill McClintock's chest. Instead of the single cross, she placed three in a diagonal line. "I win."

By the time she returned to Amanda Boom's body, the sun was kissing the horizon, and creatures of the night were singing in dusk across the desolate landscape. Who the fuck would choose to build a hotel in the desert anyway? It was no wonder the place had never been finished. Spring Gardens was dry and arid, and she could already feel the afternoon heat starting to hide away from the dead-of-night chill.

Red could hardly walk. She used an old shovel as a crutch, and she stood looking down at Amanda's body. She thought they'd been friends, as much as anyone in their line of business could be. Maybe they had been. She left her out in the open for the animals to come and eat. There were already flies on her head and ants busy making lines back and forth amongst her scattered brains.

It took Red over an hour to hobble back to her car, and as she slumped into the driver's seat she let out a deep groan. She'd need to visit a friendly doctor she knew. Have a rest. Maybe take a few months off.

Before slamming the door, she reached over and grabbed Nick Strand's head by the hair. It made a dull thump as it hit the road and rolled onto the opposite verge. It was dusk now, and she could only see it as a shadow. The head did not speak.

Red took out her phone and accessed the tracking app. She deleted Song, Amanda Boom and The Welshman, and all the lights on the app went out.

She accessed her recent calls and tapped a name.

"Dead Red Virgilio," River said. "Wasn't sure I'd ever hear from you again."

"I wasn't sure either. And it's just Red Virgilio now, if you don't mind."

"Oh?"

"I'm not dead anymore."

THE END

ABOUT THE AUTHOR

TIM LEBBON is a New York Times-bestselling writer from South Wales. He's had over forty novels published to date, as well as hundreds of novellas and short stories. His latest novel is the folk-horror *Secret Lives of The Dead*. Other novels include action thrillers *The Hunt* and *The Family Man*, the critically acclaimed fantasy series *Dusk, Dawn, Fallen* and *The Island*, the *Relics* urban horror trilogy, zombie multiverse novel *Coldbrook*, and apocalyptic horror *The Silence*, which was also a major movie on Netflix.

Tim has written extensively in existing universes, including Alien, Predator, Star Wars, Firefly and Hellboy novels. He also novelized the movies *30 Days of Night, The Cabin in the Woods, and Kong: Skull Island*. He has won four British Fantasy Awards, a World Fantasy Award, and a Bram Stoker Award for his original fiction. He was also awarded the Dragon

Award for his novel *Firefly: Generations*, and a Scribe Award for *30 Days of Night*. He has been nominated for International Horror Guild and Shirley Jackson Awards.

Tim is currently lead narrative writer on the new computer game *Resurgence* (from Emergent Entertainment). He is working with respected director Dirk Maggs as lead writer and exec producer for a major new audio drama from Audible, and he is also writing his first comic for Dark Horse in collaboration with Christopher Golden.

Tim is currently developing several more projects for audio, TV and the big screen, including scripts for his novels *Eden* and *The Hunt*. His screenplay *Playtime* (with Stephen Volk – Ghostwatch) is also in development.

Printed in the United States
by Baker & Taylor Publisher Services